MIRRORMASK

BY NEIL GAIMAN

BASED ON A STORY BY NEIL GAIMAN & DAVE MCKEAN

ILLUSTRATED BY DAVE MCKEAN

First published in the U.S.A. in 2005 by HarperCollins Publishers, New York

First published in Great Britain in 2005 by Bloomsbury Publishing Plc,
36 Soho Square, London, WID 3QY

A CIP catalogue record of this book is available from the British Library
ISBN 0 7475 8111 8
ISBN 9 780747 581116

Printed in Belgium by Proost

1 3 5 7 9 10 8 6 4 2

All papers used by Bloomsbury Publishing are natural, recyclable products
made from wood grown in well-managed forests. The manufacturing processes
conform to the environmental regulations of the country of origin.

I.

This is my story about what happened to me last year when Mum got ill and Dad and I had to go and stay at Aunt Nan's and I had my weird dream.

It's the first story I've written down, although sometimes I like to make up stories in my head. (This isn't a made-up story, though.) Normally, what I do best is draw, although I can do a lot of other things, too. I can juggle. I can sell popcorn. I can walk a tightrope and I'm an extra clown when we need one—and, trust me, the Campbell Family Circus pretty much always needs an extra clown.

I call this story MIRRORMASK, and it is written and illustrated by me, Helena Campbell.

So. Last year I had my own caravan, which wasn't big but it was mine. It had my drawings all over the walls. I love drawing places, imaginary cities with bits of all the towns the circus goes through put in them. We weren't anywhere long enough for me to go to school, so Mum would teach me things like geography and maths, and the German Tumblers taught me some German, and Eric the Violin Player used to be a biologist before he ran away and joined the circus, so he taught me science.

You probably think that with a name like The Campbell Family Circus there would be lots of us Campbells, but it's only my dad, Morris Campbell, my mum, Joanne, and me. Everyone else works for Dad. Dad says the circus is in his blood, and it was his dream to have his own circus since he was a little boy, when he learned about the first Campbell's Circus, the one my grandfather owned. He says the circus is in my blood, too.

My dad says lots of silly things like that.

Dad's the ringmaster, also he juggles and takes bookings. My mum is the brains behind the outfit. She was once a great beauty, and my aunt Nan says it was a great disappointment to everyone when she married my dad instead of going off and being a film star or something. Mum sells tickets. She talks to the bank and to the tax people, keeps the books, does things with contracts. Also she does a Spanish Web act and is the Gorilla. (Dad bought the gorilla costume cheaply when I was seven and he uses it whenever he can.)

That night Mum was utterly furious, and it was all my fault.

I'd sort of lost track of time, and I was in my caravan making up a story with my socks when my mum started banging on the window, and she's all, "Helena, you're not even dressed yet" (I *was* actually), and I was all, "Mum, it never ends. It's always smile for the punters, Helena sell popcorn, Helena juggle, Helena help with the washing up," and the washing up, even in a little circus like ours is—well, you wouldn't believe it, that's all.

"Listen to those kids in there," said Mum. "They all want to run away and join the circus."

"Let them," I said. "I want to run away and join Real Life."

After that, the argument just got worse and worse, with me inside my caravan and her outside, and I told her I was getting dressed and not to shout at me, and she shouted that she wasn't shouting, and it was all getting sort of horrid when she said, "You'll be the death of me," and I said, "I wish I was." I didn't think I'd said it loud enough to be heard, but she went very quiet. It sort of hung there in the air and it couldn't be unsaid.

"Real life? Helena, you couldn't handle real life," she said, and she went away, hurt, and I knew that this wasn't the last I'd hear about this.

I don't know what it is with me and Mum. We never mean to fight, but suddenly we're yelling at each other and it's all stupid.

I pulled on my mask, and I ran for it. The masks were my dad's idea. They make it look like there's more people in the circus than there are, so you won't go, "Oh look, that lady on the rope is the same lady I bought my ticket from." As if you'd notice, or you'd care.

I was in a rotten mood, but it started to lift when Dad and I went out to juggle (as "Raymondo and Fortuna, from Darkest Peru," and the name is Dad's. We have to talk in what I think Dad imagines a Peruvian accent sounds like). We'd just got up to the gorilla bit, where Dad says, "Hey, Bambino. You want to joggle the bananas?" and I go, "Uh-uh. You know what you get if you joggle the bananas?" and he says, "What?" and I say, "Gorillas!" and that's always when Mum comes out in the gorilla suit and chases us around the stage and then juggles the bananas.

Only she didn't. She missed her cue. And you can set your watch by my mum. And when she did come on, she didn't even try to juggle the bananas. Just ran around. But the kids were cheering, and, you know, when I ran out of the ring I was thinking that there are a lot worse things than being in a circus.

And that was when the gorilla took off its head, and it wasn't Mum. It was Fred, the strong man. Mum was on the floor. She'd passed out.

The show went on (the show must go on). An ambulance came and I watched them take my mum away. *You'll be the death of me*, she'd said, and I couldn't get it out of my head.

II.

My aunt Nan lives in a crumbling block of flats in Brighton. She says that fifty years ago it was, and I quote, "the height of modernity." Right now it looks like prison, only less inviting. Still, she's got a big flat, so I had my own room (I put my drawings up on the wall, to make it feel more like my caravan) and Dad made his bed on the sofa in the sitting room. Mum was in the hospital.

Once upon a time Aunt Nan was a magician's glamorous assistant (she says they do all the hard work while the magicians stand there and look pleased with themselves), but now she watches telly all day, goes and gossips with the other ladies in the block of flats, and loses things.

This is not, I was reliably informed,* because of old age. Mum told me that when she was a little girl Aunt Nan lost stuff, most famously a set of magical linking rings and a barometer. It was because of Aunt Nan that my mum evolved her **Two Rules for Finding Things That You've Lost**:

1) It's usually where you left it.

2) It's probably staring you right in the face.

These are extremely useful rules, by the way. It was by applying them that I found Aunt Nan's missing false teeth, in the fridge.

I finished drawing Mum's Get Well Card, I kissed Aunt Nan good-bye, and I ran for the bus. They're a bit strict about visiting hours at the hospital. I made the bus by the skin of my teeth, and I sat on the bus worrying about Mum and about Dad and about the circus. Dad and Mum are a wonderful team, but Dad on his own is . . . well, he doesn't really inspire confidence. He's got his head in the air. Mum has her feet on the ground.

*By my mum, actually.

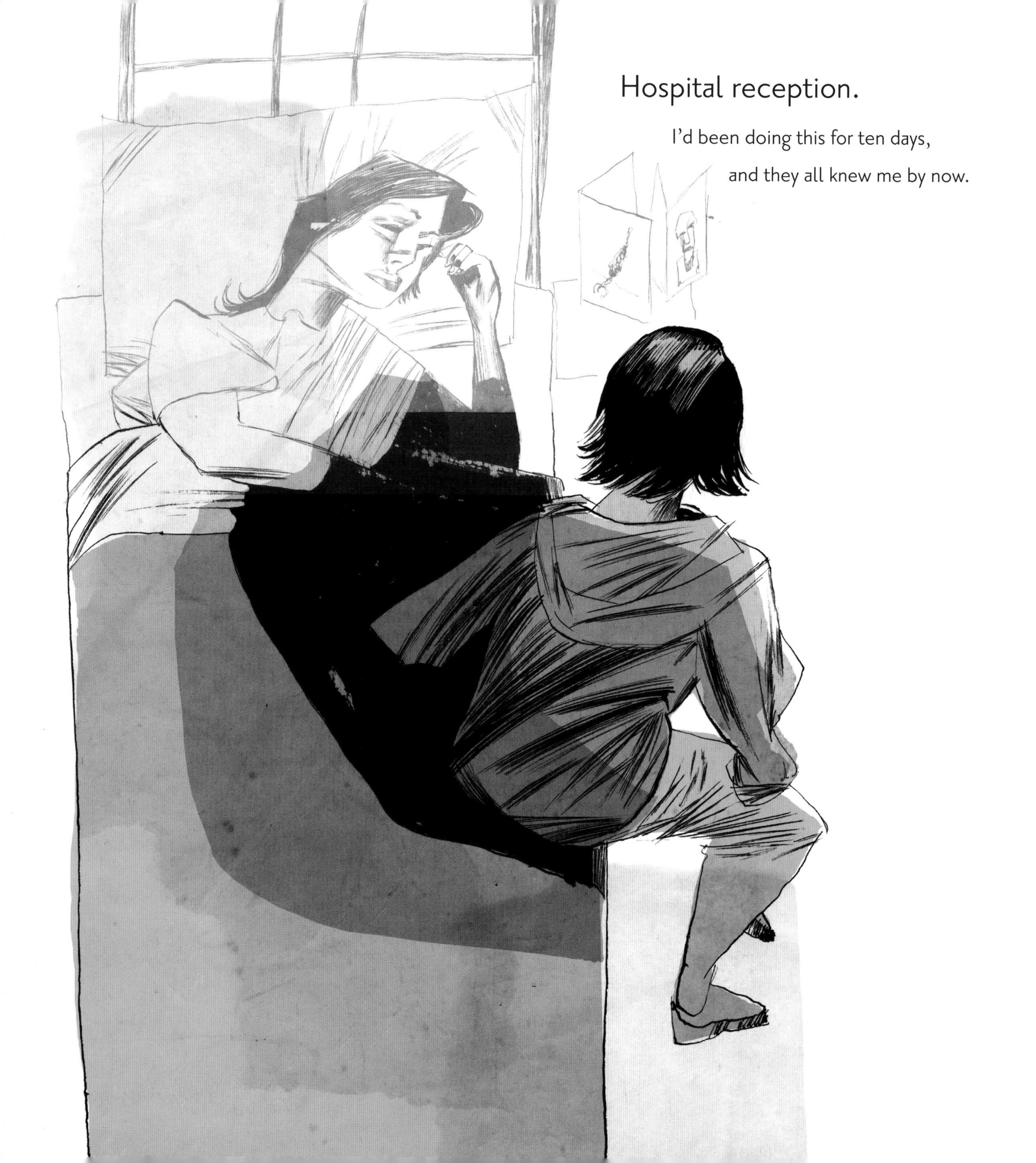
Hospital reception.
I'd been doing this for ten days,
and they all knew me by now.

The receptionist handed me a hairbrush, and then I found myself getting the third degree from the nurse on Mum's ward. They wanted to know where Dad was. I told them he was seeing the bank manager, and didn't bother saying that he was trying to borrow enough money to cover the payroll for another week off the road. I thought for one moment the nurse wasn't going to let me in to see Mum, but she did.

Mum was so white.

I gave her the card I'd made, told her the story of Aunt Nan's teeth, and she smiled, but she looked like it was an effort. Like she could close her eyes and sleep forever. I could tell that she was upset that Dad hadn't taken the circus on to Scotland. That was where we were meant to be, not off the road. Off the road is death to a circus.

"Where's your fruit?" I asked.

"They took it away," she said. "I'm not to eat anything today."

"Why not?"

"It's routine," she said, in the same way she'd told me she didn't know why Kelso The Magnificent had left the circus in Hull last season, when I happened to know:

a) that she'd fired him herself and

b) exactly why she'd fired him.

You hear a lot of things, doing the washing up, honest.

Then I said sorry, for what I said, just as I'd said sorry every day for the last nine days. I wanted her to hug me and tell me everything was okay and she'd be out of the hospital tomorrow and we'd get back on the road. But she didn't, and I went home. The wind was up now, and it was getting colder.

I let myself into Aunt Nan's flat. The living room was full of people.

They spilled out into the hall.

And in the living room I could hear my dad's voice.
"All I'm saying is that with a little time we could be back on the road,"
he said to a bunch of circus people who didn't seem very impressed,
"and I think," he added brightly, hammering the nail into his coffin,
"we could be better than ever."

I called Dad over, told him that the hospital needed to talk to him about Mum. He went and phoned, while I stood in the corridor trying to remember to breathe.

Pingo (clown, mime, contact juggler) said, "I know you always wanted off the road." Which was true, of course.

"Not like this," I admitted. "It's his dream."

"Dreams only take you so far, darlink," said Helga-from-Poland. "After that you need cash." I was too tired to argue. Helga's all right, if you don't mind someone who thinks she's cooler than you because she can do anything you can do, only upside down.

Dad came back down the corridor. "They're operating," he said. "Tonight."

That was why she wasn't allowed fruit. I felt stupid. I didn't say anything to anyone; I went to my room and got my charcoal and my chalks.

A roof is a good place to go if you need somewhere special. Up on the roof everything seems very small and a long way away, and it's just you and the sea and the sky.

I drew pictures with my charcoal: gargoyles and monsters and cats on the wall. I drew a window on the back of the wooden door, but I couldn't think of anything to draw inside it, so I started on the ground. It was going to rain soon, and so I drew a sun, certain that if I drew it properly, drew it bright enough and hot enough, it would make everything okay—it would burn away the stuff growing in Mum's head that wasn't meant to be there. I drew as hard as I could. A plop of rain hit me on the face, one of those early raindrops that turns up five minutes ahead of all the others to let you know it's time to get indoors.

"That's nice," said my dad. "What's it called?"

"It's just a drawing," I told him. "It's not called anything."

I hoped he'd just go away, but he didn't, and I heard my mouth saying, "Everybody at the hospital knew Mum's operation was tonight and nobody told me."

"They didn't want you to worry."

"Should I be worried? I mean, you said they'll operate, and then she'll be up and about again."

"Depends on what they find really, love . . ."

"What do you mean, what they find?"

"You see? Now you're starting to worry."

I got angry, then. Angry and scared. "I wasn't worried until you told me not to worry. Anyway, you're worried. You keep putting your hand on your mouth. You only do that when you're worried." And then I said it: "I shouldn't have shouted at her. It was all my fault."

Dad said, "These things are nobody's fault, love. They just happen."

It's just life. That's what he told me. We went inside.

Fish and chips for dinner. Me and Aunt Nan and Dad. Nobody said anything about Mum's operation being that night, and nobody was thinking about anything else.

I went to bed and listened to rain lash the windowpane and the rumble of the thunder until I fell asleep.

III.

In my dream, my reflection was laughing at me. In my dream, I was two different girls. In my dream, Mum was on her way to be operated on, and when she opened her eyes they were as black as glass . . .

I woke up.

The storm was over, and outside, in the road, someone was playing the violin. The flat felt deserted. I tried to turn on my bedside lamp, but nothing happened. *Power cut*, I thought. I got up, put on my dressing gown and bunny slippers, grabbed a torch, and went outside to see what was going on.

What was going on was Eric, the violinist from the circus, and he was playing the violin. I said "Eric? What's going on?"

Somebody said, "Can we please not distract our accompanist?" And I was just trying to figure out why, when the same somebody also said, "Now, we'll need a brave volunteer from the audience. You can be the brave volunteer."

"Me?"

They were jugglers, practising, juggling with glowing balls. One was tall, and the other one was talking. I sort of understood that they were jugglers. I didn't understand why they were rehearsing with Eric under Aunt Nan's flat, or why Eric was wearing a funny mask.

The talking juggler said, "What's wrong with your face?"

I didn't think there was anything wrong with it. I may not be a Great Beauty, but I've got all the bits—eyes, nose, mouth. Eric said something. He sounded like he was talking in his sleep.

"Can we have some, ohh, scary-scary juggling music here?" asked the juggler.

Eric started to play something, and then it happened. Above him a black cloud moved and shifted, so dark it swirled like a shadow against the night sky, and then the cloud reached down and—

—touched him—

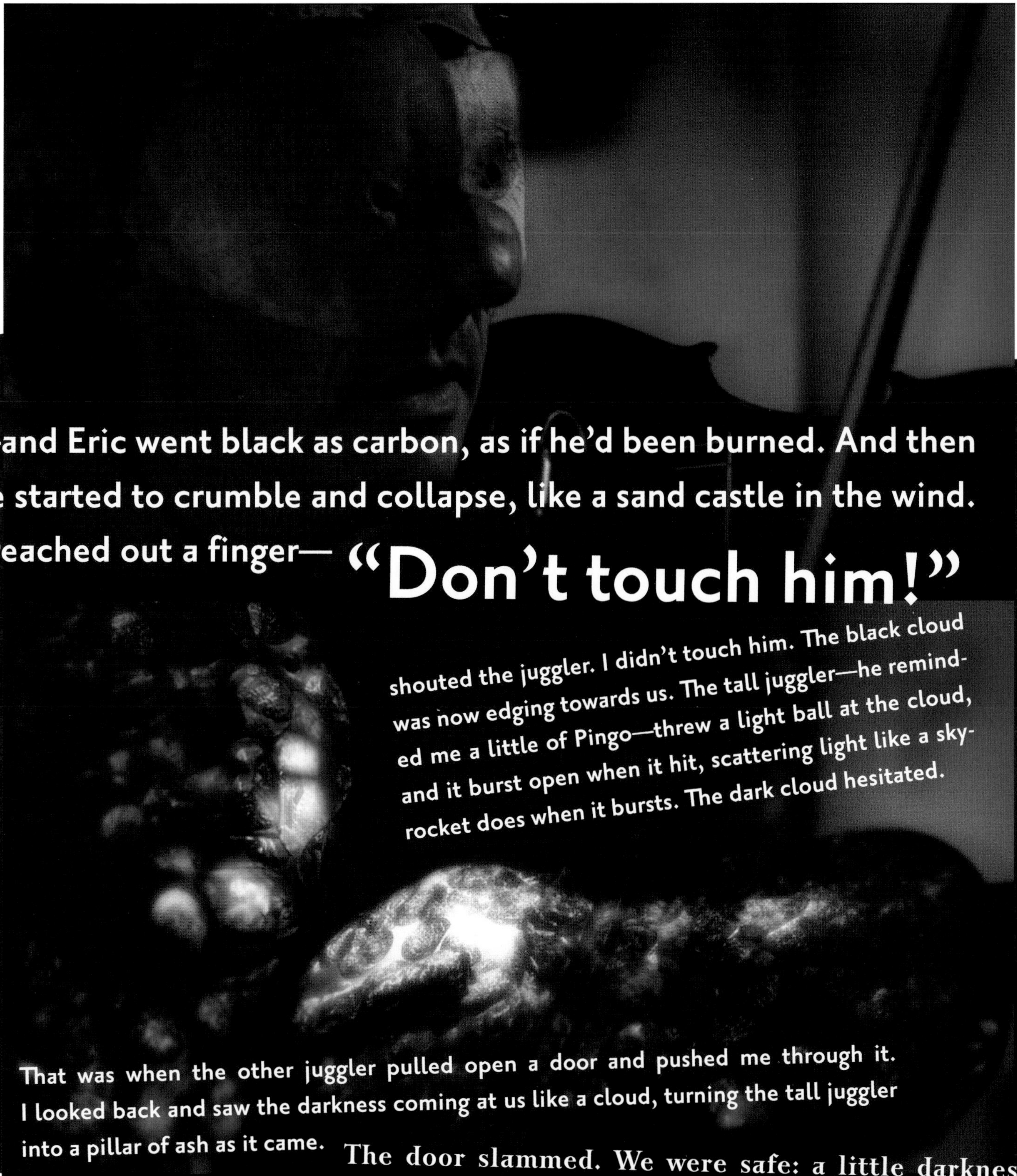

—and Eric went black as carbon, as if he'd been burned. And then he started to crumble and collapse, like a sand castle in the wind. I reached out a finger— **"Don't touch him!"**

shouted the juggler. I didn't touch him. The black cloud was now edging towards us. The tall juggler—he reminded me a little of Pingo—threw a light ball at the cloud, and it burst open when it hit, scattering light like a skyrocket does when it bursts. The dark cloud hesitated.

That was when the other juggler pulled open a door and pushed me through it. I looked back and saw the darkness coming at us like a cloud, turning the tall juggler into a pillar of ash as it came. The door slammed. We were safe: a little darkness oozed under the door, like a sooty porridge, but the door held.

"Where are we?" I asked. It looked like a junk room.

"In trouble," he said.

He was a very odd-looking person. He was wearing a mask, but it looked like his mask was his face. He wore a big flappy coat, and instead of eyes he had holes, and I was going to ask him what kind of person he was, but something that wasn't a cat came out of the corner. It had rainbow-coloured wings and sharp, sharp teeth.

The juggler seemed worried.

"Throw it a book," he said.

I threw it a book, and it tore into it, like a cat ripping a small animal apart; and while the creature ate its book the juggler pushed the door open. He nearly fell into a deep chasm on the other side. "Not a disaster," he said, as if he was trying to convince himself. "We need more books. Big books."

It didn't seem like a good time for reading, but I pulled two huge old books off the shelf in the corner and carried them over to him. He took one, but he didn't read it. He told it what a bad book it was and threw it on the ground. The book bounced in the air and hung there quivering, and the juggler man jumped onto it and began to float away. "As long as they think you don't like them," said the juggler, "they migrate back to the library. And we get a free ride."

I rode next to him on my book, and we crossed the chasm safely. The books floated away, and I waved them good-bye.

"What's your name?" asked the juggler.

"Helena."

"You ought to change it," he said. "Get a name with romance, magic, and just a hint of danger. **Something like *Valentine*."**

"What's your name?" I asked, and I wasn't at all surprised by his answer.

"Valentine," said Valentine.

He and his friend were trying to leave the city, he told me, before the shadow clouds destroyed it completely. They were a juggling act. "But where am I going to find another juggler?"

"Me. I'm a juggler."

"Of course you are," he said in that way that means I know you said something but it wasn't even worth bothering with. He started juggling—a simple cascade—so I reached out and took the ball from the air, and I showed him what I could do.

"Well," he said, "you're very boring, and you don't have a proper face. But you'll do."

And that was how Valentine and I became juggling partners.

It was also when I was arrested by beetles. Actually, looking back on it, they may not have been beetles. Whatever they were, they had long, stiltlike legs, and they clattered along the cobbles of the city like some demented caterpillar.

When you're raised in a circus you learn to spot the police, and these beetles were police if ever I'd seen them.

"If you don't mind," said a beetle.

"Could we have a word with you?" said another.

And with a couple of steps they had surrounded me. I couldn't have run away if I'd wanted to. They leaned down to look at me.

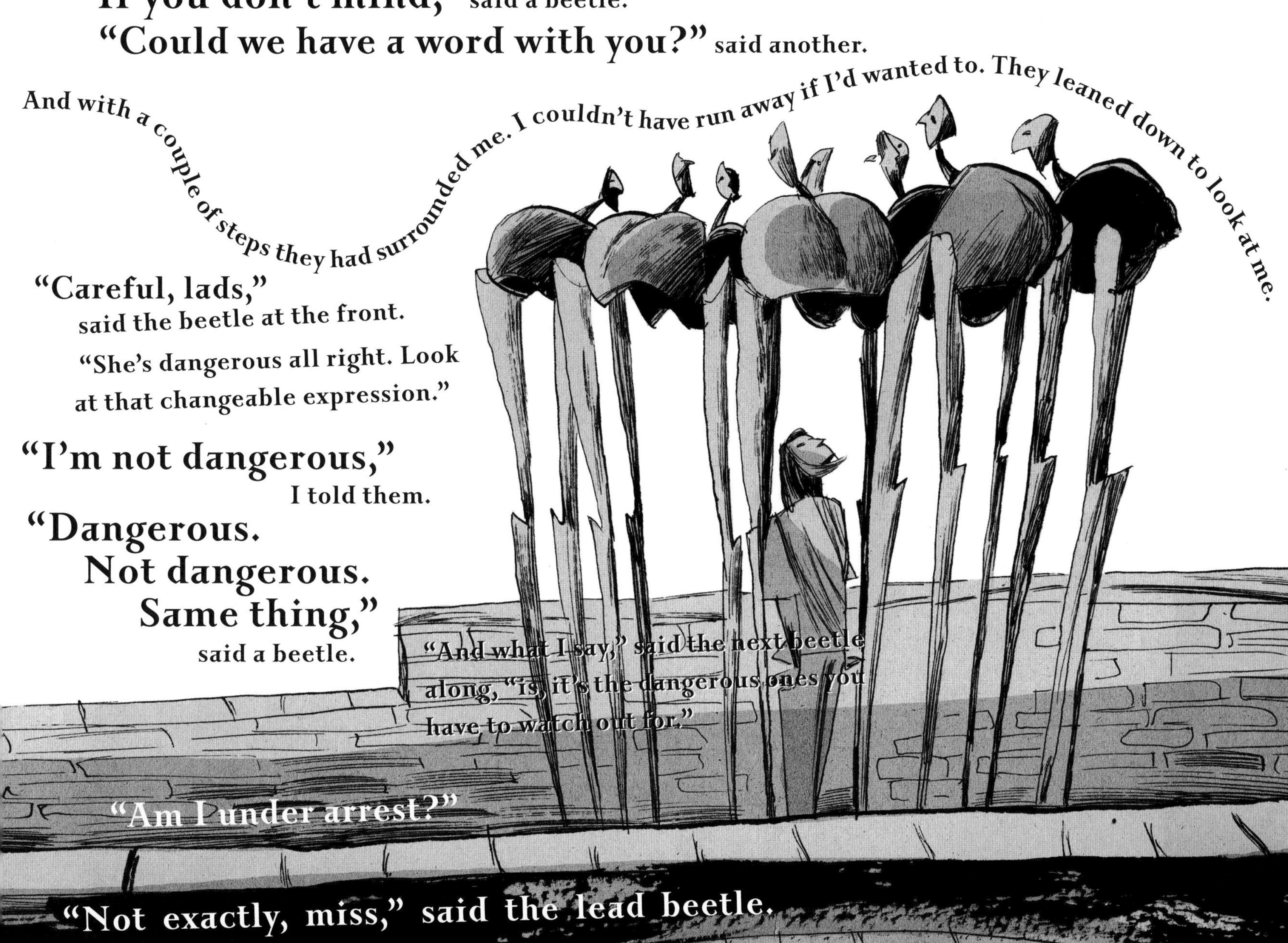

"Careful, lads," said the beetle at the front. "She's dangerous all right. Look at that changeable expression."

"I'm not dangerous," I told them.

"Dangerous. Not dangerous. Same thing," said a beetle.

"And what I say," said the next beetle along, "is, it's the dangerous ones you have to watch out for."

"Am I under arrest?"

"Not exactly, miss," said the lead beetle. "Or should I say . . .

Princess!"

And with that, they were beetling off "to the palace", carrying me with them.

And as they carried me I realised two things. (First) not to look for sense in this place, because (second) I was asleep and this was just a dream. I'd suspected it already, but as the beetle cops carried me through the city I looked through a window and saw a bedroom—my bedroom, actually—and saw me in there, fast asleep, in my bed.

And suddenly I stopped being worried. If you're in a dream, and you know it's a dream, then nothing in the dream can hurt you. Right? Well, that's what I thought at the time.

The beetles carried me into a white place that must have been the palace, and in a great hall they dropped me and retreated to a respectful distance.

"We've caught the princess, Prime Minister," said the lead beetle.

"You have? Jolly good!"

The Prime Minister reminded me of someone I knew, but I honestly couldn't have told you just who. He seemed delighted to have me in custody, anyway. "Now, young lady," he said, "I suggest you give back what you stole, or I shall be forced to stake you out for the shadows."

And I was trying to explain that whoever he thought I was, I wasn't her, when he looked me up and down, from my bunny slippers to my bed hair, and he said,

"You're not **her**, are you?"

And I told him I wasn't. I wondered who she was—obviously she looked like me, but everyone was scared of her.

"What's going on here?" I asked.

"Follow me," he said, and headed off up an enormous set of stairs, and I followed.

IV.

Everything glittered and shimmered and gleamed.

I've never been anywhere that felt as magical as that place. There were suns on the walls, and each of them shone, and on a sort of bed in the middle of the room there was a woman asleep.

She was obviously queen of that place.

On her folded hands there was a white rosebud.

Her hair was long and white, but I knew that face.

I said, but she didn't wake up.

The Prime Minister explained (with the aid of a small band of rabbits, which he kept in a box in his hat—I know how silly it sounds, but I bet you've had dreams that were sillier) what had happened:

The world was divided into two. The city of light (where we were)

and the land of shadows (which was where the shadow clouds came from).

Each place had a queen. One day a girl who said she was a princess had come from the Dark Lands to the Palace of Light. She asked for shelter and said she was looking for the Charm (whatever that was). The Queen took her in. They had a party. . . .

The next day the girl was gone, and nobody could wake the Queen. Since then, black birds and dangerous shadow clouds had started coming out of the shadow lands, tearing the White City apart. And without the Charm, the Queen would sleep on, until the city was destroyed.

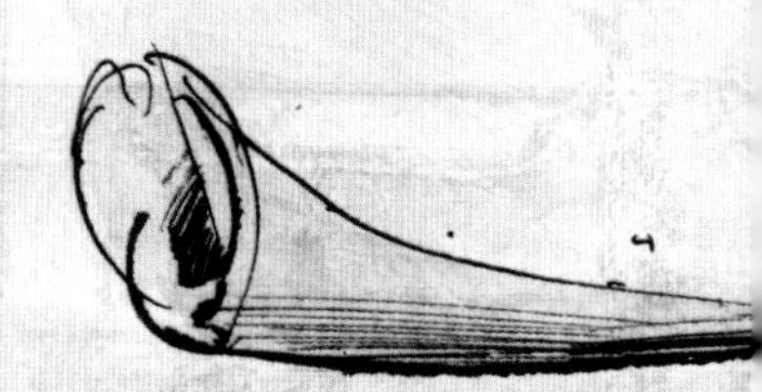

When you're in a dream, and you know it's a dream, things can seem very simple.

"I'll wake her up," I said.

I thought the Prime Minister would be happy about this, but he didn't seem very impressed. This was, he explained, because finding the Charm (whatever that was) was, as propositions go, completely, utterly, unarguably, quintessentially hopeless.

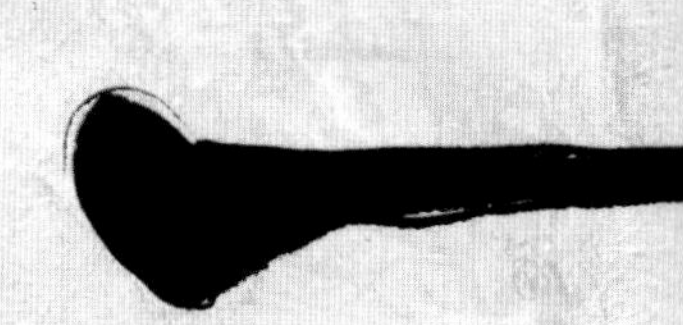

He had just finished explaining this to me when the white rosebud on the Queen's chest blossomed into a perfect white rose. "What does that mean?" I asked.

"Well,"
he conceded,

"maybe it's not *quintessentially* hopeless."

And that was how Valentine and I came to be in the library, looking for information on the Charm (whatever that still was) and how to wake the Queen. And on what this place was. Valentine liked the idea of being on a quest. "How big's the reward?" he asked.

"The reward is, we wake the Queen and save the world."

"No treasure? As your manager I would have made sure that—"

"You're not my manager," I told him.

"We can sort out the contractual details after we find the Charm."

There was a grumpy librarian in the library. I could tell that he was the librarian, because he seemed to be made of books. I told him that we needed information, and he got us some butterfly nets and sent us up to the top floor of the library.

I wondered why we were carrying nets. Valentine didn't know.

The book I wanted was pretty obvious. It was called

A HISTORY OF EVERYTHING.

Finding it was easy. Catching it, however, was not. The moment I reached for it, the whole shelfful of books took off into the air, **fluttering like pigeons,**

and suddenly I knew what the butterfly nets were for.

I waved the net about, and eventually I caught A HISTORY OF EVERYTHING. As soon as I'd got it, all the rest of the books flapped back to their shelf, all except one, a little red-covered book, which fluttered over my head happily.

The librarian read to us from the history. It seemed to be all about a girl who had made the world by drawing it. It was filled with sentences like *The Charm she placed beneath the sign of the Queen, to show the city that she knew it would never be finished, because the city was her life and her dream, and it would live forever.* And I was in the middle of trying to understand that, when I realised I'd made a new friend. The little red book had come to rest on my shoulder.

The cover of the book said

A REALLY USEFUL BOOK. I opened it.

A sentence was written on each page, odd things like MOST GHOSTS ARE SCARED OF WHISTLES and TRY DANCING. Valentine looked at the book.

"'WHY DON'T YOU LOOK OUT OF THE WINDOW?'" he read. "That's not useful."

I looked out of the window. The White City was spread out beneath me. A little way away I could see a park in the shape of the sun.

"The sun is the sign of the Queen, isn't it?"

I said. "I think we just found a place to start."

The librarian said, "You'd better take the book with you. If you leave it behind it'll just depress the rest of them, and before you know it they'll start molting. Pages everywhere."

Somehow I didn't believe that he was anywhere near as grumpy as he pretended to be.

We walked through the streets, while Valentine wittered on about treasure and how he was a **Very Important Man** and how he Owned a Tower, and I noticed something extremely odd. When I looked through windows, I saw my bedroom at Aunt Nan's house. But I wasn't there. The room was empty.

"Shouldn't I be there," I asked, "if I'm dreaming?"

"You're dreaming?" said Valentine, surprised.

"Well, yes. I think we've rather definitely established that."

"Well, it's not a bedroom," he said, looking through the window. "It's somebody's front room."

“H
You shall

We reached the park. There was a sign over the gate: GIANTS ORBITING—ENTER AT YOUR OWN RISK.
"Sounds a bit iffy, doesn't it?" said Valentine, and he sat down.
"I'll see you when you get back."

Some manager, I thought. I was only just through the gate when a creature with an almost human face bounded over, showed its teeth, and said,

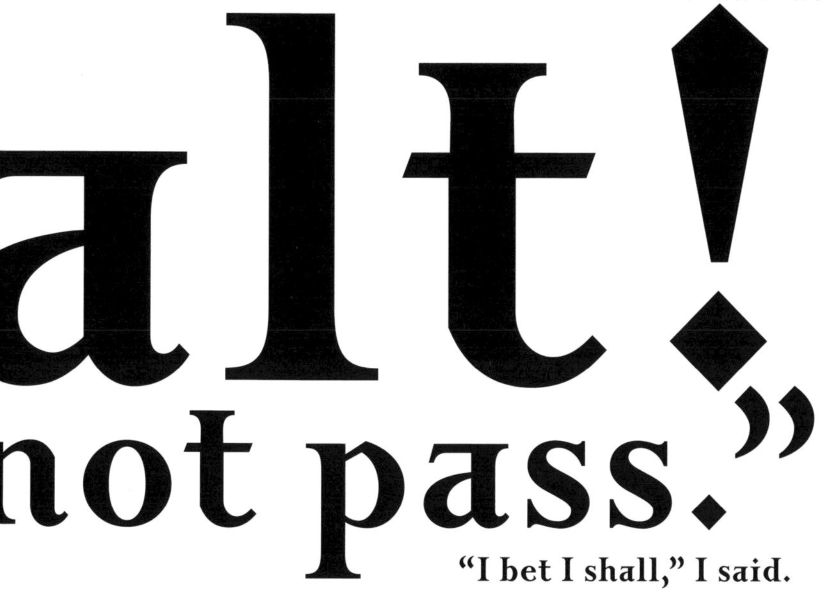

"I bet I shall," I said.

"Answer my Riddle, and only then you can pass. Fail, and I devour you, bones and all! What walks on four legs in the morning, two legs in the afternoon, and three legs in the evening?"

Well, that was pretty obvious. I'd seen it happen the week before, after all.
"William. He's a performing dog."

The gryphon thing licked its lips. **"No. The answer is—Man!"**

"I think you'll find it's William, actually. I saw him. He walked on four legs in the morning, on two legs during the afternoon show, and he was limping on three legs at night, because he hurt his paw. And he can skateboard. My go. What's green, hangs on the wall, and whistles?" It was a riddle of my dad's. I nearly kicked him when he told me the answer, but it was the only one I could think of. "Give in?"

It looked irritated. **"No. Let me think about it."**

I said, "You have a good think. I'll be back in a bit."

There was something in the sky: a lumpy sort of mass, like a statue the size of a ship. I walked towards it, and it drifted towards me. When it got closer, I could tell that it was indeed giants and that they were orbiting. From what I could tell, they were a man and a woman, who looked as if they had been carved out of stone a long time ago and weathered down. They were pressed together: the woman looked as if she was going to float off into the sky, and the man was being pulled down towards the ground; so as long as they were together, they floated in the air.

Valentine came puffing up, muttering that we were in danger. I decided that the wisest course of action was to ignore him, and I climbed up the nearest tower.

"We are looking for the Charm, to wake the Queen," I shouted. "Can you help us?"

When the male giant spoke, his voice was so deep that it made my stomach tickle.

"Many . . . have . . . asked . . . where . . ."

"Many have asked where the Charm is, yes?" said Valentine, who felt that this ought to move a little faster.

"the . . ."

"the Charm is . . ." asked Valentine.

"Charm . . ."

"is?"

"is."

Valentine was tugging at my sleeve. The giant carried on.

"We . . . guard . . . the . . ."

"Charm?" said Valentine.

"box . . ."

And I could see it. The lady giant was holding something in her hand, a little silvery box. I could see something else, as well. Shadows were squirming through the sky like the tentacles of some enormous octopus. "That was what I was trying to tell you," exploded Valentine. "If he doesn't get to the end of this sentence in the near future, we are dead." "for . . . the . . . Queen."

Now the shadow tentacles had reached the giants. The male caught one in his hand, snapped it off, and dropped it to the ground. And more shadows came. And more. Too many for them to break off. Too many for them to fight.

The lady giant spoke.

Charm is . . . the Mirror . . . Mask . . ."

she said. And she passed me the silver box.

I grabbed it and we ran.

By the time I was at the bottom of the tower, though, it was already too late. The giants had been parted by the darkness. Now the female floated off into the air, while the male crashed to the ground like a man falling into a swimming pool: it swallowed him and rippled and froze again, and they were gone forever.

Poor things.

V.

In the silver box was a key. Valentine was not impressed. "We just have to try the key in every single lock we pass," he said, "and when we find the one that key opens, we'll know that ten thousand years have gone by."

That was when the gryphon thing turned up again, and I told it the answer to the riddle. (No, I'm not going to tell you what it was. It's a very silly riddle, indeed. But the gryphon let us go, so that was a good thing.)

"So what sort of thing is a—a MirrorMask?" I asked.

Valentine scratched his head. "It's a . . ." He stopped and said, "I think we should ask somebody who knows."

"Such as?"

"Such as the people in there," he said, and pointed to a run-down shop at the end of the street.

It said MASK SHOP.

So we went inside.

There were masks on the shelves and masks on the walls, and some of them looked at us and smiled and winked as we came in, but they were pretty dusty and the shop didn't look like people came there and bought masks very often. (Why would they, I wondered, when they all had masks of their own already?)

"Yes, dears? Can I help you?" The woman—I learned later she was called Mrs Bagwell—was as old and as dusty as her shop. She looked as if bits were flaking off her. "I was just about to have tea. Do you like cakes? Oh, you young people, it's all tea and muffins and excitement in your world, I expect." And she took us back into her sitting room, to have tea and cakes.

The sitting room was dusty, too, and every spare space was occupied by one of the little cat things, the sphinxes with the sharp teeth. They watched us with cruel little eyes.

I hadn't realised how hungry I was until I saw those cakes. There were dozens of them, and each one looked nicer than the one next to it. And I was about to tuck in, when she told me to go and wash my hands.

The bathroom in that house was the dirtiest place I think I've ever been. I washed my hands in cold water, dried them on my dressing gown . . .

Movement caught my eyes from the window in the corner, and I went over to it, wiped at it, and saw . . .

Me.

Only she wasn't me.

She wasn't wearing the kind of clothes I'd wear. And she was screaming at my dad. He looked scared, and tired. I hated that she was shouting, that he didn't tell her to behave, that he was backing away from her.

I banged angrily on the window. The girl who wasn't me turned, and for a moment I was certain that she was actually looking at me.

I stumbled back to the sitting room, to watch Valentine eating the last of the cakes, while Mrs Bagwell talked about the little sphinxes. ". . . the kittens do the funniest things. My husband, the late Mr Bagwell, thought they were a nuisance. He called them moggies. They loved him, though. They were so upset after he disappeared that they wouldn't touch their food for a week. More cake, dear?"

"I haven't had any yet."

"Well, you must force yourself."

"Look," I said, "we need to know about the MirrorMask. We thought you might know something about it, having a mask shop."

"There was a girl about your age over here not long ago. She was asking about it. I'll tell you what I told her. Now let me see. . . . Mr Bagwell used to say the MirrorMask concentrated your desires. Your wishes. It would give you what you needed. I remember I said to him, 'Mr Bagwell, how can a mask know what you need?' And he said, 'Cynthia, remember, I don't know what I'm talking about.'"

And she obviously didn't. I checked the REALLY USEFUL BOOK as Mrs Bagwell went to get some more cakes.

DON'T LET THEM SEE YOU'RE AFRAID, it said.

"Don't let who see you're afraid?" asked Valentine.

The sphinxes grinned at us with hungry little mouths and showed us their sharp little teeth.

Out in the alley behind the house I saw my first wanted poster with my face on it. It was me, but it wasn't me. She looked like a princess.

"Why do you keep saying you've got a tower?" I asked Valentine.

"Because I have. It's huge. **Enormous.**
Hundreds of rooms. Stairs. Doorknobs.
A scullery . . . possibly more than one scullery, actually."

"And I can't see it because . . . ?"

Valentine looked uncomfortable.
"We aren't talking.
The tower and I had a . . . minor disagreement. And it left without me.
I said something stupid and it flew off without me."

"Why don't you find it and say you're sorry?"

"I wouldn't give it the satisfaction.

Heap of rubble.

Anyway, I don't know where it is.
Up there somewhere.

Anyway.

Valentines
Never
Apologize."

And that was when the cat things approached us.

"Hungry,"

said one of the sphinxes, and it grinned at us.

I gave them my cakes,
and we started to back away,
and then stopped backing away,
because they had us surrounded.

"What do we do now?"

"I don't know," admitted Valentine.

I didn't know how we were doing at not letting them see we were afraid.
I looked at the REALLY USEFUL BOOK.

Valentine looked doubtful. "What does it say?"

I showed him: **MY PAGES TASTE EXCELLENT BUT ARE STICKIER THAN TOFFEE AND VERY DIFFICULT TO CHEW.**

Valentine looked disgusted. "What an appalling book. That's the most useless thing it's told us so far."

"No," I told him. "It's a very brave thing to say." And I ripped the pages from the book and threw them down for the sphinxes. They tore into the pages as if they were the best sweets in the world, and then began chewing, their mouths gummed together by the pages of the book.

We ran, then.

VI.

There's a park on the borderlands, between the city of light and the wilderness of shadows. It's a dream park.

I'm not sure that I can describe it properly. It looks like dreams.

I was certain it was the place where we'd find the MirrorMask. We passed strange buildings (through a window I saw the girl who looked like me in my bedroom, talking to a boy. I didn't like the look of him. He was just dodgy. He was eating chips from a newspaper. And then he sat down next to her, and they started to kiss. It was disgusting. He was disgusting. He didn't even put down the chips) and finally, at the center of everything, there was a pool.

"These are the dreamlands," said Valentine.
"It's not a proper place.
It's made of wishes and hopes.
We often confuse what we wish for with what is.
Well, I know that I do.
Did you see that?"

I hadn't seen anything. "What?"

"Up there. My tower."

"No," I told him. "I didn't see anything."

He sat by the pool and started skimming pebbles across it.
I tried to understand why the place was so familiar.

I was somewhere that looked like my bedroom at Aunt Nan's, only it was empty. I was standing there, trying to remember what I was doing.

My mum said, "Honestly, love. What have you lost now?"

She didn't look like my mum. She looked more like the White Queen.

"I was looking for a MirrorMask, but I don't know what it looks like or how big it is or why it's missing or anything, really."

"Well, where did you last see it?"

"I don't think I ever have." I think we were on a bus then. I'm not sure. It was the only bit of my dream that actually felt like a dream, really. Things blended and swam.

"I want to come home now," I told her. "I want you to be okay. I'm scared, Mum."

"I'm scared, too, love," she told me. "That's why I'm having this dream. Do you think they've started to operate yet? Maybe everyone gets dreams like this when they start poking around in your head."

"It's not your dream, Mum. It's mine." I think we were in a hospital then. Or maybe we were in the palace. I don't know any longer.

"That's the kind of thing people say in dreams. I wish your dad was here." And then she noticed Valentine, skipping his stones in the pool. "Hullo. Did I dream you a boyfriend?"

"You did not! He's a—he's just a—he's not—"

She smiled. "I'm sorry I brought it up. Now, you're looking for something, you know it's here, you can't find it. So look again. I'll bet it's just like Aunt Nan's teeth. It's probably staring you in the face."

And I knew then where it was. Well, sort of.

Because it was **my** dream, not hers.

And if it was my dream, then I'd put a little building—a little white dome—in the middle of the pool—just like I'd done when I drew this place. It was on my wall, and in that drawing, it had a little dome in it. So I knew it was there . . .

. . . and because I knew it was there, it was. Valentine followed me across a bridge that hadn't been there a few seconds before.

"You're not my boyfriend," I told him. "Even if this is my mum's dream."

Inside the dome was a huge column, filled with keyholes. I took out the key, tried it in one of them. It didn't work.

There was also a little window. And when I looked through it, I saw that girl again, the one who looked like me. And she was looking in at us through the window. And then she reached out and . . .

. . . everything lurched and crashed. It felt like the dome had been ripped out of the world and was now being carried (in the hands of a girl who looked just like me, I thought) through the air (or across my bedroom) and then, with a crash—

—dropped, in the Dark Lands.

It was pretty scary, and when we fell, I hurt my arm.

"You stay here," said Valentine. "I'm going to fetch help."

"I'll come with you."

"You're hurt. Stay here. Don't move."

"But what about you?"

Valentine preened. "Oh, I'm a panther," he said. "I shall slip unnoticed through the darkness like a dark unnoticeable slippy thing."

And suddenly I felt ever so grateful, and a bit guilty for thinking that he was so dodgy. "That's really nice of you. I know we haven't always got on, but I'm really grateful for all your help. I couldn't have done any of this without you."

"I do my best," he said. And he was gone.

I sat on the floor and rubbed my arm. Through the window I could see the other Helena sitting on the bed. She was smoking a cigarette. She was holding one of my drawings. And then she lit a match and touched the flame to the picture.

Through the open door I saw a pillar of flame on the horizon.

Back in my bedroom, my dad had come in. He started telling her off. And he took the matches away from her.

I banged on the window. I shouted,
"Dad! She's not me . . .
. . . oh, Dad . . ." but I knew he couldn't hear me. I wasn't so certain about her, though.

I was angry and upset and scared, but at least I knew Valentine was off getting help. I just hoped he'd be quick about it. Right now, the girl-who-wasn't-me was tearing the world apart, a little bit at a time, because she could.

Something made a noise outside the dome. I thought it was Valentine and looked out. They were tall and black, like armoured things with nothing in the armour. They held a huge net, and before I could say a word I was wrapped in the net. It was like being dropped into a web of darkness, and in the darkness I shouted and shouted but nobody heard me at all.

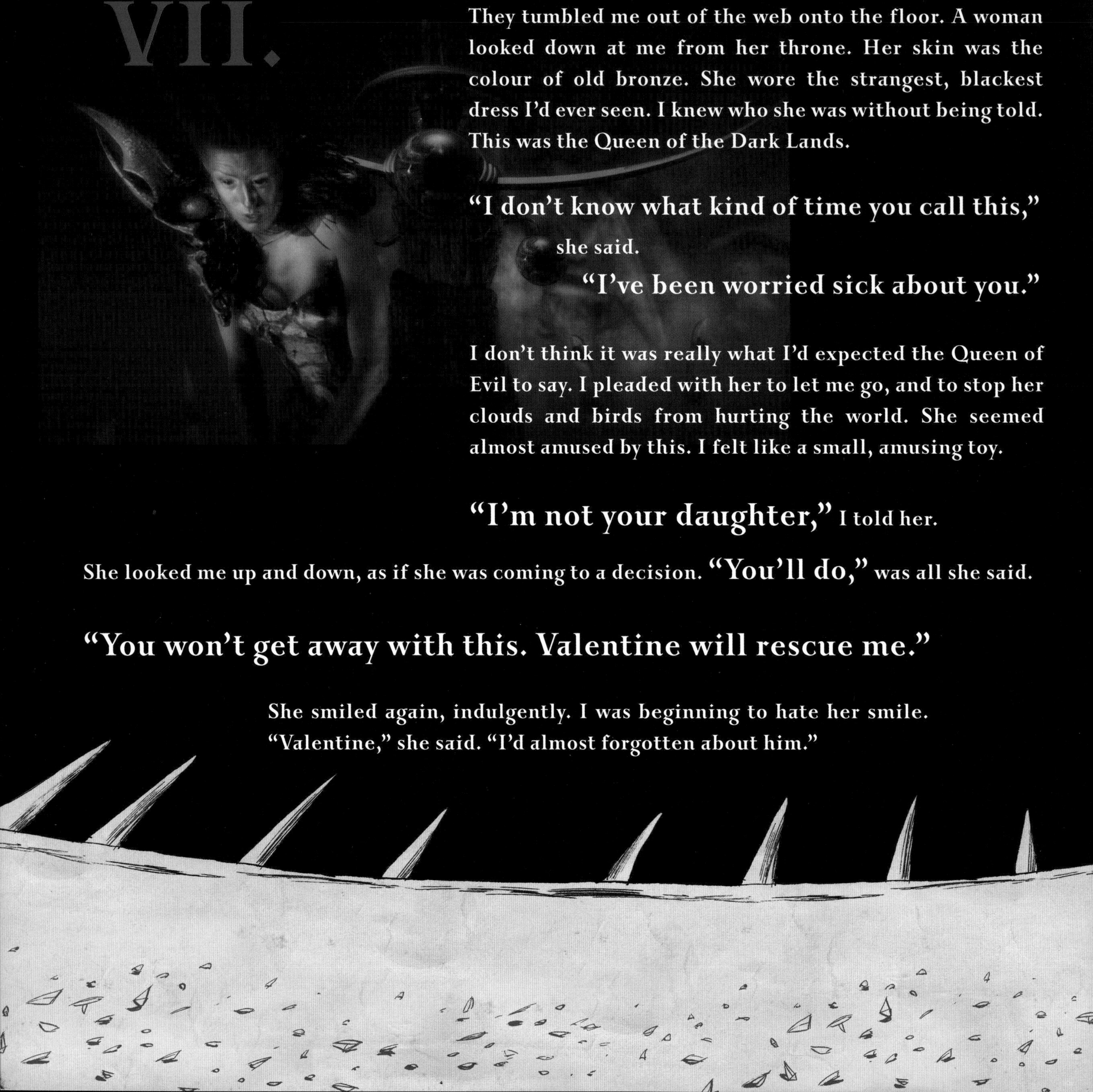

VII.

They tumbled me out of the web onto the floor. A woman looked down at me from her throne. Her skin was the colour of old bronze. She wore the strangest, blackest dress I'd ever seen. I knew who she was without being told. This was the Queen of the Dark Lands.

"I don't know what kind of time you call this," she said. "I've been worried sick about you."

I don't think it was really what I'd expected the Queen of Evil to say. I pleaded with her to let me go, and to stop her clouds and birds from hurting the world. She seemed almost amused by this. I felt like a small, amusing toy.

"I'm not your daughter," I told her.

She looked me up and down, as if she was coming to a decision. "You'll do," was all she said.

"You won't get away with this. Valentine will rescue me."

She smiled again, indulgently. I was beginning to hate her smile. "Valentine," she said. "I'd almost forgotten about him."

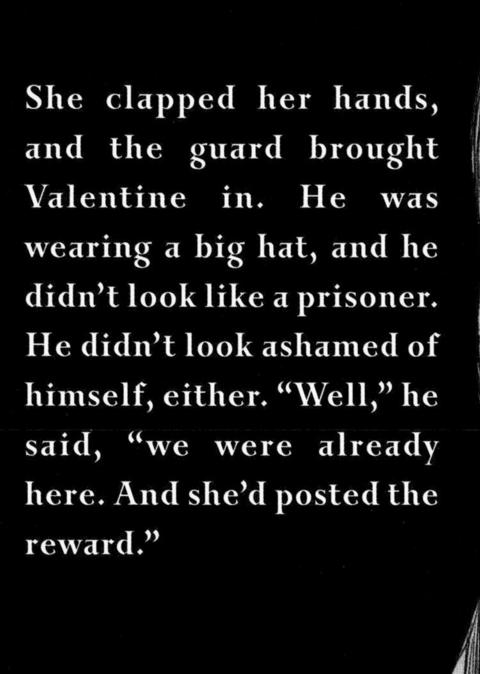

She clapped her hands, and the guard brought Valentine in. He was wearing a big hat, and he didn't look like a prisoner. He didn't look ashamed of himself, either. "Well," he said, "we were already here. And she'd posted the reward."

I hated him. I don't think I've ever hated anyone quite as much as I hated him then. My eyes stung.

Dark jewels tumbled across the floor,

and he swept them up in his hands and his hat.

He filled his pockets.

He looked at me.

"So—no hard feelings, then?"

"Throw him out,"

said the Queen to her guards, and I was glad she did. I never wanted to see him again.

I think I was crying then.

The Queen touched my cheek with her hand. "Do you know what you need?" she asked.

"I need to get away from here.

I need to go home.

I need to find the Charm.

I need to wake the White Queen.

I need—"

"You need a pretty frock," she said, oblivious. "And a happy smile. With a smile on your face everything will seem a lot brighter, because we are—

what?"

"I don't know."

"We are not at home to Mister Grumpy."

I was at home to Mr Grumpy, not to mention Mr Hopeless, Mrs Furious and Miss Despair, but I followed her down a corridor. "This is your dressing room," she said. A door opened. She pushed me in, and I heard the door lock behind me.

The room was filled with drumlike boxes. I had the mad idea that inside each of the boxes was some kind of jack-in-the-box; and then the tops of the boxes opened and I discovered that my mad idea was the truth: dolls came out of them, made of metal and string and old bits of clockwork, and they were the most beautiful and scary things I'd ever seen.

They were singing to me. I wanted to run away, but the air was filled with a glittery golden dust, and suddenly I was a million miles away, watching the world through the wrong end of a telescope. That was how it felt. I might have been at the other end of the universe: things were happening to me, but they might as well have been happening to someone I barely knew.

I watched them as they took me, and they made me beautiful. It was like I was another girl, and I watched her clothes, her hair, her lips, as the dolls made her perfect. She was me, and yet she wasn't me at all. She wasn't angry. She didn't feel anything at all.

She opened her eyes, and they were black as glass.

She wasn't me anymore. They had made me into the thing the Dark Queen wanted me to be—perfectly passive and, looking back on it, perfectly pathetic.

My life became something that pleased the Queen. I did what she wanted. I stood behind her, sat beside her. I played with dolls.

And all the time the world continued to fall apart.

There were no windows anywhere in the Dark Palace, so I couldn't look out. But after lunch each day I would be sent out to the steps to play with my ball, and then I could see flames on the horizon, and once a patch of sky vanished, as if it had simply been ripped.

In my bedroom—the princess's bedroom—was a looking glass, and it had two eyeholes in it, so that the Queen could watch me from her throne room when I was sitting on my bed. I was pleased she watched me. It made me feel loved.

Family dining was incredibly important to the Dark Queen. She sat at one end of the table and lectured me on etiquette, and I sat at the other, and I ate and said, "Sorry, Mama," when I'd done something wrong.

Everything shook.

I wondered if it was an earthquake.

Mama frowned. Then she opened her mouth wide, threw her head back, and coughed out two black bird shapes.

"Go," she said. "Be my eyes. Find out what's happening."

Etiquette demanded that I offer to help. I said, "You know what's happening. She's going to destroy everything. Your real daughter. When she left, she threw this whole world out of balance, and now it's falling apart."

She looked angry.

"You will not talk to me like that!"

"No, Mama. Sorry Mama. Can I have some more ice cream, please?"

She smiled, and relaxed. I was happy.

"Good girl. Just one scoop, though."

I was no longer worried. My mama knew everything, and she would take care of everything. I ate my ice cream, and a million miles away I sat outside my head waiting for the end of the world.

There was no day and no night in the palace, but my life as a princess was divided into periods: I'd wake, I'd eat, I'd play with my toys, I'd study a large book called 17,011 THINGS A PRINCESS MUST KNOW (it had a whole chapter on cutlery), I'd sleep.

After lunch, I went out to the steps to play with my ball.

That was what I was doing when the man came.

I'd dropped my ball,
and it had bounced down the steps.
He picked it up.
I didn't know who he was:
it wasn't one of the 17,011 things a princess must know. He wore a flappy coat.

"I suppose that an 'oops and I promise not to do it again'
isn't actually going to cut the mustard," he said.

The princess who was Helena who was me sort of looking
down at him from a long way away didn't say a word.

"You were right and I was . . . not as right as you were. About everything. The MirrorMask. The windows. The world ending.
The whole bit. And you probably hate me. I mean, I'd hate me, too."

"Look, whatever she's done to you . . . I know you're still in there."
It was a funny thing to say. I wasn't in there. I was so far away.

He sighed. "Oh well," he said. "Onward and upward."

Then he threw the ball back to the princess at the top of the stairs who was me, and I caught it. And then, because it was etiquette, or because the girl was lonely and it's not much fun playing with a ball on your own, I/she threw the ball back.

And he caught it, and tossed it back to me. Then he added another ball in. The toss became a cascade became an intricate weave of balls and lights.

She owned my head, the Dark Queen, but she didn't own my hands, and they remembered how to juggle. They remembered, and they pulled me back from a million miles away.

The juggler dropped a ball, and I heard a voice saying something a princess would never have said. It was my voice. It said, "Butterfingers."

And Valentine was looking at me with an expression on that funny, mask face of his I'd never seen before. I was me. I was more me than ever.

VIII.

I knew where the MirrorMask was. I'd figured it out, from my time as a princess. Her bedroom, like my caravan, like my bedroom at Aunt Nan's, was her refuge. It was where she went when things got bad. It was where she stored her treasures. When the Queen wasn't spying on her, it was where she kept her secrets.

If the MirrorMask was anywhere, it was there. I was sure of it. Because it was where I would have hidden it. And there was some level on which she was me. I knew that now.

I snuck Valentine up to the princess's bedroom, and we looked inside every drawer, on top of everything, underneath everything, while Valentine told me about going back to the dome, with his pocketful of jewels and his new hat, and trying the key in every lock until he found the right one. And when it opened, in the compartment, he found, not the MirrorMask, but a letter.

He showed me the letter.
It was in my handwriting. It said:

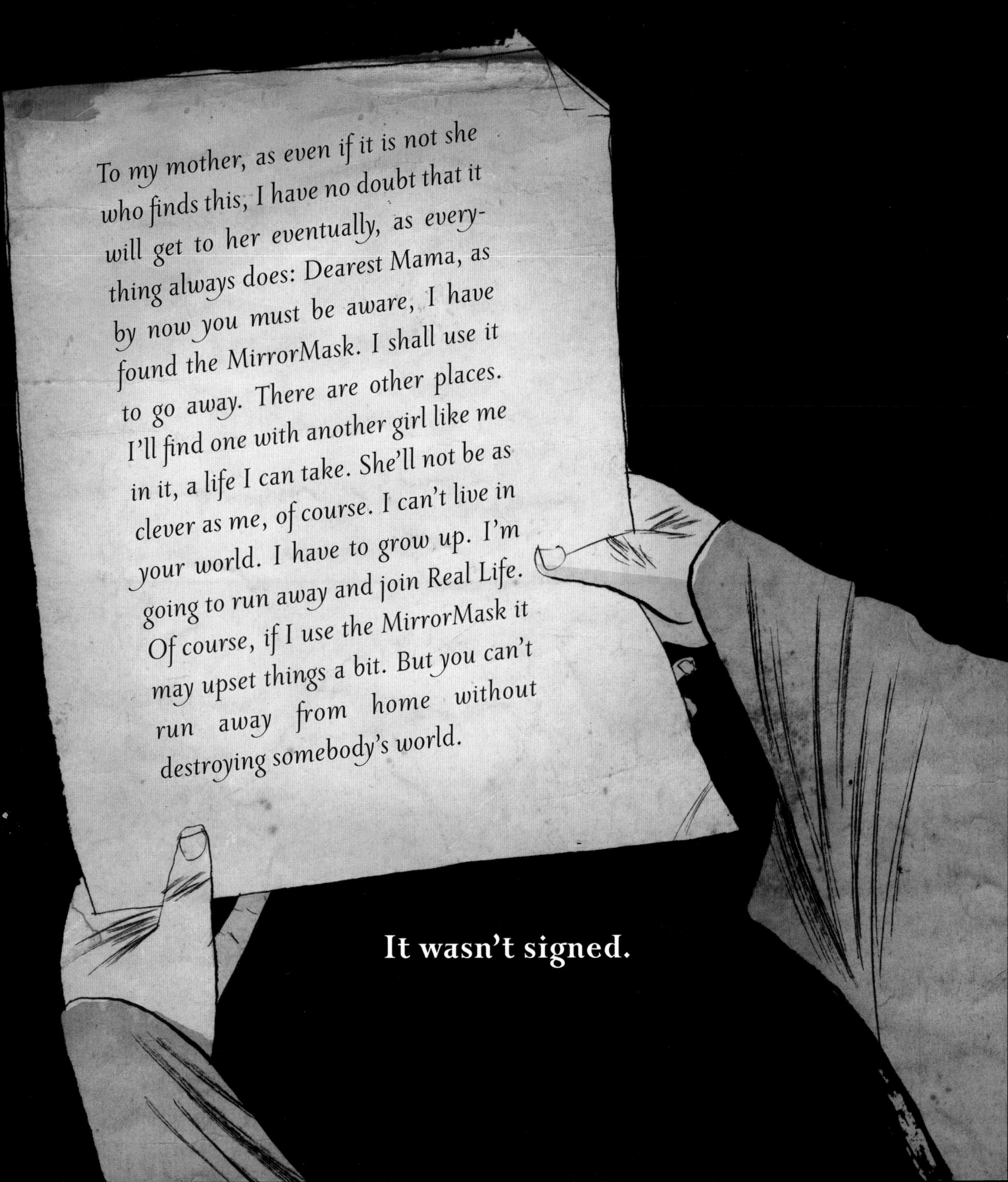
To my mother, as even if it is not she who finds this, I have no doubt that it will get to her eventually, as everything always does: Dearest Mama, as by now you must be aware, I have found the MirrorMask. I shall use it to go away. There are other places. I'll find one with another girl like me in it, a life I can take. She'll not be as clever as me, of course. I can't live in your world. I have to grow up. I'm going to run away and join Real Life. Of course, if I use the MirrorMask it may upset things a bit. But you can't run away from home without destroying somebody's world.

It wasn't signed.

I wasn't worried about the Queen spying on us. Eyeholes work both ways, and I could see through the holes in the mirror. She was receiving a delegation of odd, lumpy-looking creatures, complaining about the destruction that was happening. ("The Swamp of Doom simply isn't there anymore! It was a lovely swamp. You can't get them like that these days.")

"I am going to call a council,"

announced the Dark Queen, and she banged a gong. Good. That would keep her busy for hours.

I sighed.
"We've wasted so many opportunities.
We don't even have the REALLY USEFUL BOOK . . ."

Valentine took the battered remains of the little book out of his pocket and tossed it into the air.

It flapped over to me and settled on my hand.

There was only one page left.

What if it's the wrong page? I thought. Then I opened the covers and I read,

"REMEMBER WHAT YOUR MOTHER TOLD YOU."

"What does it say?" asked Valentine.
"'Remember what your mother told you.'"

He nodded. "Mine said, 'it's a dog-eat-dog world, you get them before they get you, eat your greens, please don't do that, don't embarrass me in front of the neighbours,

I think it will be better for everyone

if you leave home and

please don't ever

come back.'"

I didn't know what to say.

"She wasn't actually my mum, either," he added. "She bought me from a man."

I started trying to explain to Valentine about my mum and her Two Rules for Finding Things That You've Lost.

1) It's usually where you left it.

2) It's probably staring you right in the face.

But the only thing that was staring me right in the face was me, in the looking glass over the bed. I looked at it. A girl dressed as a princess looked back at me, dejected and tired. And then she didn't look anywhere nearly as dejected anymore. It was obvious.

It had been staring me in the face all the time.

"Valentine," I said, "are you thinking what I'm thinking?"

"Absolutely," he said. "If we put little wheels on our feet we could just roll around everywhere."

"No, silly. What's the best place to hide a mirror?"

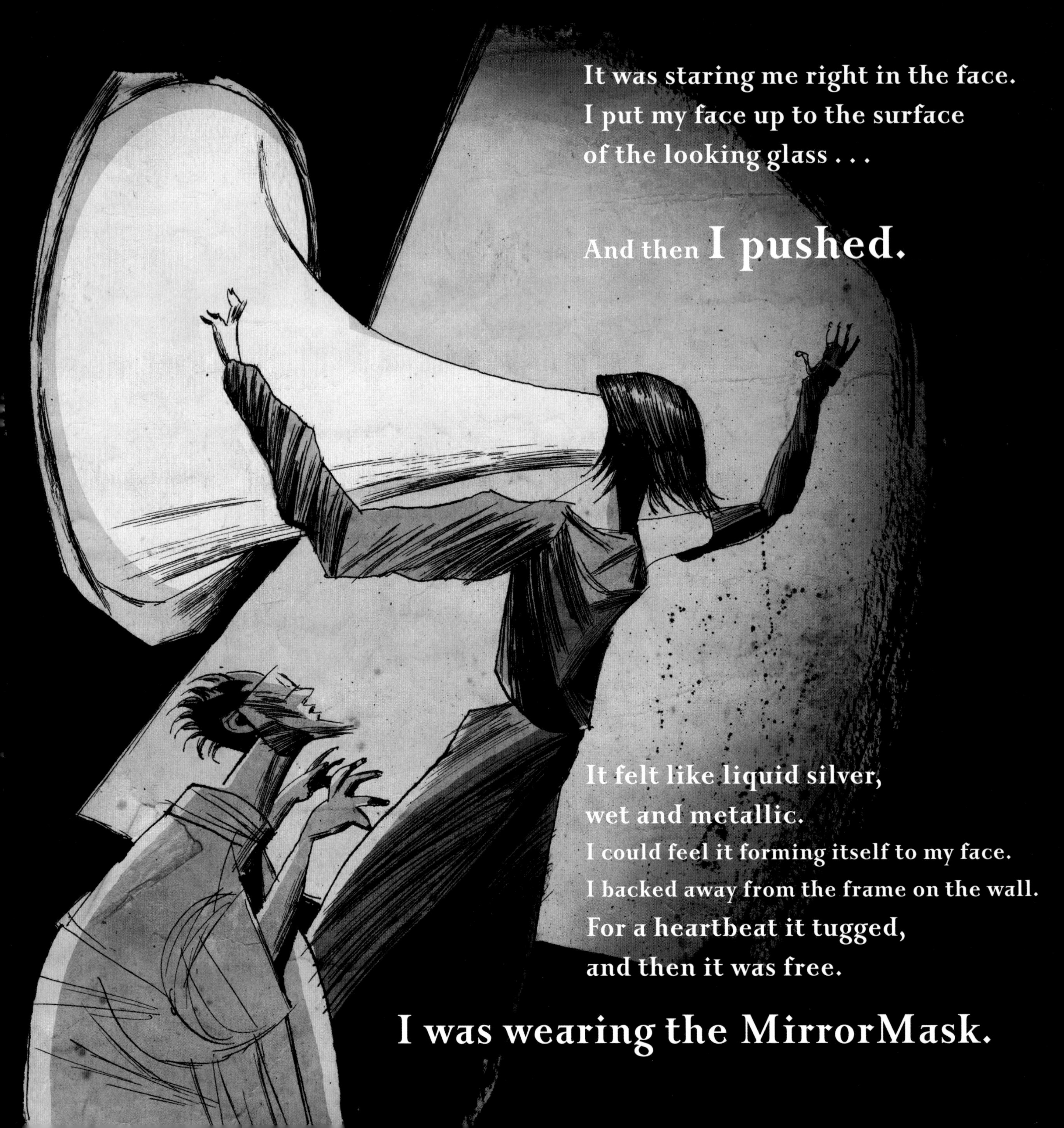
It was staring me right in the face.
I put my face up to the surface
of the looking glass . . .
And then **I pushed.**
It felt like liquid silver,
wet and metallic.
I could feel it forming itself to my face.
I backed away from the frame on the wall.
For a heartbeat it tugged,
and then it was free.
I was wearing the MirrorMask.

It was weird.
I still remember how when I had the mask on I knew things.
I knew that I had to bring the other girl back,
if I had any hope of waking the White Queen.

I knew something else, too.

If I wanted to, I could get out.

It wouldn't take me to my own world, but it would give me what it had given her.
Another world. Another girl like me to displace.

It would be a way out.

And I couldn't do it.

I kept thinking of that letter that Valentine had found:
you can't run away from home without destroying somebody's world.
She was right.
It's not hard to mess things up.
It's a lot harder to try and put the world back together again.

And if I was going to do that,
I was going to need to find a window.
I had to see her.

So we ran for it. Along empty corridors, through a great door, and down a hundred steps. We ran through the dark forest, panting for breath, our hearts pounding in our ears; and if ever I slowed or stumbled Valentine would shout,

"Keep running! Don't stop! Keep running!"

Until, in a clearing, he shouted,

"Food!" and he stopped.

It was an enormous fruit growing in the middle of the forest, bigger than the tree it grew upon. It looked like an orange, or perhaps an apricot. "Valentine!" I said. "We don't have time! The moment the Dark Queen realises I'm gone she'll be after us!"

"You're completely right," he said, and he peeled the fruit, ripped at the rind.

A small woman, who had been asleep at the foot of the tree, came over to me gingerly and asked, "Excuse me, but is he very holy?"

I was pretty certain I knew the answer to that one. "No. Why?"

"Well, you're meant to be holy, to eat the future fruit. The fruit takes hundreds of years to grow. And when it's ripe, a holy person comes and eats the fruit, and when they return they write whole books about it."

Valentine was now scoffing the fruit (which was a lot smaller, now the peel was gone). "It's yummy," he said. "Why do they call it the future fruit?"

"Because that's where you go when you eat it, my honey," said the woman.

Valentine looked as if he was about to tell her how stupid she was, when he flickered and blinked out of existence completely.

He wasn't anywhere.

And then he was.

He had his hands over his face, and he was trembling.

"Noooooo!"

he wailed.

"I don't want to be a waiter!"

I grabbed him, before anything else could happen, and pulled him back into the woods. We ran.

"What was that about, then?"

He sort of explained as we ran. He'd seen himself—he'd really travelled into the future, and had taken the MirrorMask from me, and used it to go into my world. He'd tried working as a street juggler, but the police had moved him on, so he got a job as a waiter. It was, from the way he described it, a nightmare of mixed-up orders, unhappy diners, and dropped plates.

I wondered if he'd learned any kind of lesson from this. Probably not. I don't think Valentines learn lessons.

We kept running. I could see the way out of the shadow lands, the broken towers of the White City on the horizon. Behind us, a pillar of fire flared and flamed.

"She's destroying the world," I told Valentine. And she was. Also snogging boys, eating chips, smoking, and fighting with my dad.

IX.

And now we were out of the forest and running across a barren plain. My heart rose. We were nearly there. In the White City there would be windows by the dozen. I tried to run faster, tripped on the hem of my dress, and went flying.

Princess dresses obviously aren't made for running in. I was ripping the bottom half of the dress off when a shadow fell across the ground in front of me, and a voice loud as thunder said,

"I should have known you'd be involved in this, Valentine."

Her head was the size of a city, and she stared down at us from the sky.

I said,

"Listen to me. Your daughter is going to destroy everything. I need to find a window and get back there. Please, let us go."

"You are my daughter."

"You know that's not true."

The black-glass eyes stared down at us. She spoke in a reasonable tone of voice, and the ground shook.
"You come back with me.
I'll execute Valentine humanely.
And we'll say no more about it."

I had to get it across to her.

"Your real daughter. She's not a pet.
She's not even a child anymore. You have to let her grow up."

"You mean . . . let her choose her own clothes. Her own food.
Make her own mistakes. Love her, but don't try to possess her?"

She was getting it, and I knew we were still in there with a chance.

"Yes," I told her. "That's exactly what I mean."

The face in the sky pursed its lips.

"Absolutely out of the question,"

it said, and it opened its mouth.
Darkness spewed out of her lips and poured towards us.

Valentine muttered, "I don't need this, you know. I'm a very important man."

"If we can't get away from her, you're a very dead man."

He grunted. "The thing you have that makes light. Where is it?" I gave him the torch.
He turned it on. "And the mask. Give me the MirrorMask."
I hesitated. "For heaven's sake. I know what I'm doing!"

I gave him the mask.

He shone the torch directly onto the MirrorMask, and it beamed a beacon of light straight up into the sky. The shadow tendrils backed away from the light—at least it made that happen. It didn't seem to be doing anything else, though.

"It should have been here by now," said Valentine. "That was always our signal."

"What are you talking about?"

"The tower. I told you, I've got a tower."

"I thought you said you'd had an argument."

"Only a difference of opinion. And I was **completely** in the right."

"**Sometimes,**" I told him, as the darkness swirled closer and closer, "you just have to say you're sorry."

It's more than that, and I think by then I knew it. It's more than saying sorry. It's meaning it. It's letting the apology change things. But an apology is where it has to begin.

"I'm sorry!"

Valentine shouted at the sky, and he meant it.

It was the size of a small skyscraper, and it dropped from the clouds like a, well, like a building dropping from the sky, hurtling down towards us until it was only a few feet away, and then it touched down as lightly as a snowflake just in front of us.

It opened its front door invitingly, and we raced inside. Tendrils of shadow came at us, but the tower crashed up and away and into the sky, and in moments we were out of the Queen's clutches.

And we even had a window. Valentine looked out of it. "She's crumpling up the world!" he told me. "Look at the ground." I couldn't see what he was seeing. When I looked through the window, I could only see a girl who looked like me. By the look of the pile of papers on the bed, she'd taken almost all of my drawings down from the walls already.

"Quickly, Valentine! Give me the MirrorMask."

He pulled it out, and he hesitated. Valentine looked at the MirrorMask, and there was a greedy expression on his masky face. It was as if I could watch him thinking: the world is ending. There is only one way out. Even if it does lead to being a waiter . . .

It was a l o n g m o m e n t.

And then he gave me the MirrorMask.

Too late.

With a smile on her face, the other girl, the not-me, reached out her hands towards us, and she crumpled the world into blackness and nothing. The window showed only blankness, like static.

"It's over,"

I said. And I knew it was the truth.

"She's won."

There are things you can get in dreams you can't do in real life. In my dream, I was seeing through her eyes. I felt her anger, her triumph, her fierce unholy joy at destroying the world she came from. I rejoiced as she (I) crumpled the last of the sheets of paper that had once held her world.

Her lips (my lips) whispered,

"I'm never going back."

I took the drawings, went into the sitting room to get the matches, got glared at by the old busybody for my trouble, and then headed up to the roof.

At least up there they wouldn't yell at me.

Out of the flat and up onto the roof and the wind was blowing so hard the matches wouldn't catch, but the same wind that blew out the matches carried the drawings out to sea as scraps and confetti as she threw them—as I threw them—up into the air.

And triumph is in her head and it's intoxicating. She won. She beat them. She outsmarted them all, from Mama in her palace to the soppy goody girl she displaced. She tricked them and she beat them,
and nothing could ever make her go back, not ever again.

It was perfect.

The girl on the roof laughed with joy, laughed and laughed and laughed until the wind caught the door to the roof and **slammed it** closed with a bang.

That was when she saw the window I'd charcoaled on the back of the door.

She was me, too, in the window, looking at her. I was holding the MirrorMask. Her face fell.

"I'm not going back!" she said.

"You can't make me."

Her words, but it was my voice. **"I like it here."**

"It's my world," I told her. "My life. And you can't have it."

The wind blew, up on the roof, and she looked very small and very alone. I don't think life as a sort of doll prepares you for very much except for running away. She said, "I just wanted a real life."

"Real life?" I told her. "You couldn't handle real life."

And I put on the MirrorMask.

It was like being in the eye of a hurricane: the world swirled and shook around me, but I was fine. I could feel her being pulled towards me, being pulled into the window. For a moment I couldn't remember which one of us I was.

It's a lot like being some kind of god, when you wear the MirrorMask. Or it's like writing a book. You can fix things, or you can sort of do something in your head and let them fix themselves. It's not hard.

With the MirrorMask on, I could see everything:

The White City was restored and its towers and spires shone in the newly minted sunlight.

The White Queen opened her eyes.

The Queen of Shadows reached out a hand to her daughter (who was still, in some way, me), who hesitated, then held it tightly. They had another chance to get it right, and I hoped this time they'd take it . . .

. . . and I understood everything, wearing the MirrorMask. The shadows and the sphinxes and the floating giants, the floating books and the riddles and the fish in the air—

—it all made utter sense.

Trouble is, I don't remember *how* it made sense, because that's when I noticed that Dad was shaking my shoulder and telling me to wake up.

"Funny place to go to sleep, love," he said, and I opened my eyes.

I was still on the roof, but it was morning.

"I wasn't asleep . . . I was in . . ." and for a moment, I couldn't remember where I'd been. I only sort of remembered being on the roof, I knew that. Then I remembered everything, and I said,

"Mum!"

"No news yet, love. Let's just keep our fingers crossed.

Look at you. You must be frozen . . ."

He put his coat around my shoulders.

He was right. I was cold.

Dad's phone rang, and I found it and passed it over to him, and he talked to the people at the hospital, talked so low I couldn't even hear him. Normally, I can read my dad, but I didn't know what to think. He looked like he was on the edge of tears. *Please*, I thought. *Please, please, please.*

He closed the cover of his phone.

"Well? What did they say?"

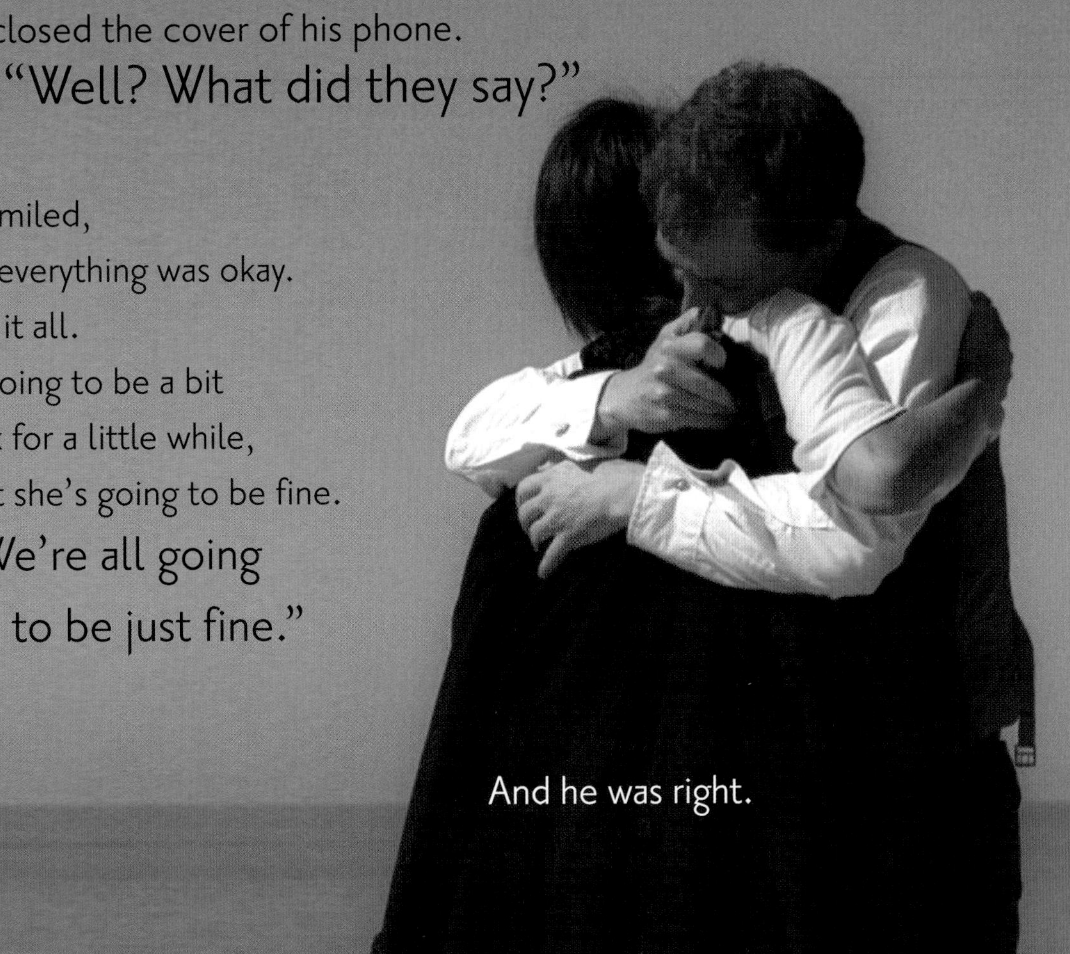

And then he smiled,

and I knew everything was okay.

"They got it all.

She's going to be a bit

weak for a little while,

but she's going to be fine.

We're all going

to be just fine."

And he was right.

X.

We've had our ups and downs since then, but that's what families have, ups and downs.
Dad took the circus back on the road—Mum joined us in Aberdeen.
She's not doing the Spanish Web or the Gorilla, though.
And Dad's agreed to me going to art college in a few years.
Sooner or later, he's going to need a new juggler.

I still remember that night, and that dream.
Sometimes when I see cats,
I expect them to have human faces and sharp teeth and little wings.
And I always put my books down carefully, in case they fly off or just bounce
in the air and go back to the library.

There's only one thing I'm missing from my life right now,
and I'm pretty sure he's out there somewhere.
I mean, there was a me in that world and a me here as well.
So I'm pretty sure I'll find him, if I keep my eyes open.

And there's one thing I know about him.
I'm not sure what he's called in this world,
and I don't actually even know what he looks like with a real face on.
But if I keep my eyes open, I know I'll bump into him one day.

After all, he really doesn't want to be a waiter.

HELENA CAMPBELL

CAMPBELL
FAMILY
CIRCUS
MIRRORMASK

Neil Gaiman is the author of the bestselling children's book CORALINE and of the picture books THE WOLVES IN THE WALLS and THE DAY I SWAPPED MY DAD FOR TWO GOLDFISH, illustrated by Dave McKean. He wrote the script for the film *MirrorMask* and is also the author of the critically acclaimed and award-winning novels and short stories for adults, as well as the *Sandman* series of graphic novels. Among his many awards are the World Fantasy Award, the Hugo Award, the Nebula Award, and the Bram Stoker Award. Originally from England, Gaiman now lives in the United States.

Authors photograph by Vanessa Kellas

Dave McKean is the director of the film *MirrorMask*. He has also created illustrations and photographs for many CD, book, and comics covers, and is best known for his graphic novels, including the bestselling ARKHAM ASYLUM and Neil Gaiman's *Sandman* series. He also illustrated the children's books CORALINE, THE WOLVES IN THE WALLS, and THE DAY I SWAPPED MY DAD FOR TWO GOLDFISH and is the author and illustrator of the award-winning graphic novels CAGES and PICTURES THAT TICK. He has written and directed several short films, and contributed production designs for the second and third Harry Potter films. He lives in England.

For more information about the author and illustrator visit www.gaimanmckeanbooks.co.uk

POST SCRIPT
Gryphon: What's green, hangs on a wall and whistles, remember?
Oh. Right. Yes, that one. So you give up?
Kind of. Not really. I mean, I'm sure I'll know it when you say what it is.
Okay. It's a herring.
But a herring isn't green!
You can paint it green.
But a herring doesn't hang on a wall!
You can nail it to a wall.
But a herring doesn't whistle!
Oh, come on. I just put that in to stop it from being too obvious.